OUTFOXED

By Mike Twohy

A PAULA WISEMAN BOOK
Simon & Schuster Books for Young Readers
New York • London • Toronto • Sydney • New Delhi

For Linda, with love

SIMON & SCHUSTER BOOKS FOR YOUNG READERS

An imprint of Simon & Schuster Children's Publishing Division • 1230 Avenue of the Americas, New York, New York 10020

Copyright © 2013 by Mike Twohy • All rights reserved, including the right of reproduction in whole or in part in any form.

SIMON & SCHUSTER BOOKS FOR YOUNG READERS is a trademark of Simon & Schuster, Inc.

For information about special discounts for bulk purchases, please contact Simon & Schuster Special Sales at 1-866-506-1949 or business@simonandschuster.com.

The Simon & Schuster Speakers Bureau can bring authors to your live event. For more information or to book an event, contact the

Simon & Schuster Speakers Bureau at 1-866-248-3049 or visit our website at www.simonspeakers.com.

The illustrations for this book are rendered in markers and colored pencils. • Manufactured in China • 0713 SCP

2 4 6 8 10 9 7 5 3 1

Library of Congress Cataloging-in-Publication Data

Twohy, Mike. • Outfoxed / Mike Twohy.—1st ed.

p. cm. • "A Paula Wiseman Book."

Summary: Fox breaks into a henhouse to steal a chicken for dinner but grabs Duck, instead—a clever fowl that pretends to be a dog.

ISBN 978-1-4424-7392-8 (hardcover) • ISBN 978-1-4424-7393-5 (eBook)

[1. Foxes—Fiction. 2. Ducks—Fiction. 3. Humorous stories.] I. Title.

PZ7.T9314Fox 2013 • [E]—dc23 • 2012026356

first edition

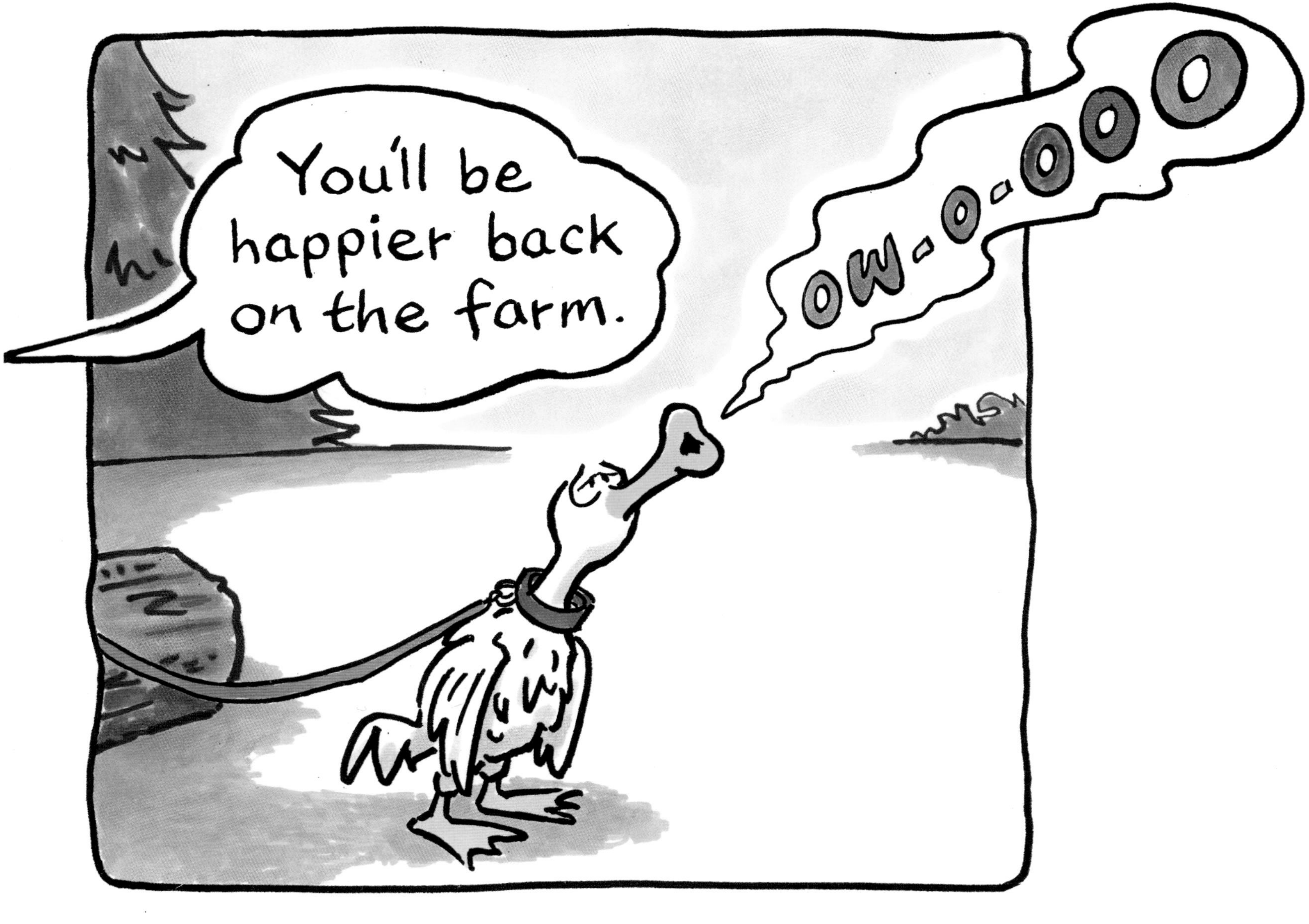
You'll be happier back on the farm.
OW-O-OOO